Forever Friends

Come Explore with Drag and Rex:

2: Sweet and Silly

Forever Friends

Susan Lubner   illustrated by Blythe Russo

PIXEL INK

To my husband and forever friend, David
—S.L.

To Madison and Zoey, my forever buds
—B.R.

Text copyright © 2023 by Susan Lubner
Illustrations copyright © 2023 by Blythe Russo
All rights reserved

Pixel+Ink is an imprint of Holiday House Publishing, Inc.
www.pixelandinkbooks.com
Printed and bound in June 2024 at Leo Paper, Hershan, China.
Book design by Jay Colvin

Library of Congress Cataloging-in-Publication Data

Names: Lubner, Susan, author. | Russo, Blythe, illustrator.
Title: Forever friends / written by Susan Lubner ; illustrated by Blythe Russo.
Description: First edition. | New York : Pixel+Ink, [2023] | Series: Drag and Rex ; 1 | Audience: Ages 5–8. | Audience: Grades K–1. | Summary: Best friends Drag and Rex could not be more different, but together they find joy and adventure in the simplest places.
Identifiers: LCCN 2023015724 | ISBN 9781645951155 (hardcover)
Subjects: CYAC: Best friends—Fiction. | Friendship—Fiction. | Dinosaurs—Fiction. | Tyrannosaurus rex—Fiction.
Classification: LCC PZ7.L9682 Fo 2023 | DDC [Fic]—dc23
LC record available at https://lccn.loc.gov/2023015724

Hardcover ISBN: 978-1-64595-115-5
Paperback ISBN: 978-1-64595-119-3
E-book ISBN: 978-1-64595-117-9

First paperback edition, October 2024

3 5 7 9 10 8 6 4

This book was printed on FSC®-certified text paper.

Contents

Full of Surprises

Chapter 1: Breakfast Buddies　　　　　　1
Chapter 2: Castle Cake 6
Chapter 3: The Ghost 12

Winter Fun

Chapter 1: Snow Day 20
Chapter 2: Almost a Snowbear 26
Chapter 3: Fun at Last 32

The Scary Story

Chapter 1: Shhhh! I'm Reading 40
Chapter 2: A Monster-ish Dragon 46
Chapter 3: Maybe Scary, Maybe Not 50

Full of Surprises

Chapter 1

Breakfast Buddies

In a small house (but big enough for a T. rex and a dragon), tucked far inside the big woods, lived two great friends.

"Why are you staring at the eggs?" Drag asked Rex.

"I don't know what to make for breakfast," Rex answered. He closed the refrigerator door.

"I'll help you decide!" said Drag. "I'm good at deciding."

Rex would have raised his eyebrows in surprise if he *had* eyebrows. Instead, he smiled politely. "I will fry the eggs."

"But you fried eggs yesterday," said Drag. "Then I will boil them."

"That takes too long," said Drag. "Fine. I'll have cereal."

"Boring!" said Drag. He pretend-snored, and a flame shot out from his nose. The loaf of bread on the counter turned to ashes.

"I guess I won't be making French toast," Rex said with a sigh. "I know. I'll make blueberry pancakes!"

"Nope," said Drag.

"Why not?"

"Because I ate all of the blueberries."

"I don't like *plain* pancakes," Rex grumbled.

"Oh, I know that! But you love chocolate chip pancakes . . . ," Drag reminded him.

"Yes!" said Rex. "Chocolate chip pancakes will be very tasty!"

Drag hung his head. "But I ate all of the chocolate chips, too."

Rex crossed his tiny arms.
Drag crossed *his* big arms.
"Let me think . . . ," said Rex.
"I'll help you think . . . ," said Drag.
"Hmmm . . . ," said Rex.
"Hmmm . . . ," said Drag.

After a while, Rex finally said, "I'm not eating breakfast."

"Why not?" Drag asked.

"Because it's time for lunch. Peanut butter?"

Drag grinned. "I'll get the jelly!"

Chapter 2

Castle Cake

In the kitchen, Rex tied on his apron. "Let's bake a cake for Lilly Pop. We can use the eggs I didn't eat for breakfast," he said.

"Is it Lilly Pop's birthday?" Drag asked.

"No, it's not."

"Then why are we baking her a cake?"

"Because it's nice to surprise friends," Rex explained.

"Oh, okay," said Drag.

Rex mixed the butter and sugar together.

Drag measured and dumped flour into a bowl. Next, he stirred in milk. "This reminds me of playing with sand at the beach. I'm good at making castles." Drag stuck his claws into the batter and tried to make a tower.

"Drag," said Rex. "What are you doing?"

"I am making a castle cake."

"That's not how you make a castle cake," said Rex.

"You're right. We don't have a drawbridge!"

"No, that's not the problem." Rex grabbed a clean sponge and mopped up the small mess his friend had dripped all over the countertop.

"First, we need to mix all of the ingredients together. Then we will use a special pan to make a castle cake."

Drag scratched his head. "Don't you have to make the castle first then put it in the pan?"

Rex showed Drag how it was done.

When the castle cake was ready for the oven, Rex set the timer.

"Surprising a friend smells good," Drag said, watching the pan through the oven door.
He checked the timer every few seconds until finally . . . *DING!*

"Careful! Don't get too close—it's very hot," Rex said as he pulled the cake out of the oven. "It needs to cool before we frost it."

While the cake cooled, Rex went into the den and practiced the piano.

Drag peeked at the cake.

Rex read his book in his comfy chair by the fireplace.

Drag sniffed at the cake.

Rex added three rows to the scarf he was knitting.

Drag poked at the cake with his claw.

"It's time to frost the cake!" Rex said. "I love surprises!" he called out to Drag as he walked into the kitchen.

"SURPRISE!" said Drag.

Chapter 3

The Ghost

"I'm sorry I ate Lilly Pop's surprise castle cake," Drag said.

"I'm sorry you did, too." Rex sighed. "We can give her the scarf I'm knitting instead."

"A scarf doesn't taste as good as cake," said Drag.

"Then I won't need to worry about you eating it." Rex added a log to the fire, sat down in his favorite chair, and picked up his knitting.

"Is the scarf done yet?" Drag asked.

"Not yet," said Rex.

"Is it now?"

"Be patient, please."

"How about now?"

"Drag . . ." Rex dropped his knitting onto his lap. "Find something to do!"

Drag toasted a marshmallow with his breath.

He played smoke-ring toss.

He caught snowflakes on his tongue outside the window. "I'm not good at waiting," he said after a while.

"Why don't you tell me a story?" Rex suggested.

"I see a ghost!"

"That's a good start!" Rex counted his stitches.

"It's getting closer!"

"Keep going," Rex said, finishing the very last row of scarf.

Drag pointed. "It's here!" He flapped his wings in a panic.

THUMP, THUMP! There was a loud pounding on the door.

Drag tried to hide under the coffee table.

"It's not a ghost. It's a snowy Lilly Pop!" said Rex, welcoming her inside.

Lilly Pop hopped up and down to shake the snow off her long ears. "For you," she said holding out a box for her two friends.

"What's in there?" Rex asked.

"Look and see."

Drag was so excited, he almost knocked the box out of her hands when he lifted off the top.

"Surprise!" said Lilly Pop.

"A carrot cake!" Drag said. "My favorite!"

"Surprise to you, too!" Rex wrapped the scarf around Lilly Pop's neck.

"So warm!" Lilly Pop smiled. "Thank you!"

In the kitchen, Lilly Pop sliced three pieces of cake, being very careful not to get frosting on her pretty scarf.

"Delicious!" said Rex.

But Drag didn't say a thing. He couldn't. His mouth was too stuffed with cake.

Winter Fun

Chapter 1

Snow Day

"Hurry up and get ready!" said Drag, tossing winter clothes out of the hall closet. "I can't wait to play in the snow!"

Rex rummaged through the pile for his warmest things. "It's a perfect day for making a snowbear!"

"Rex," said Drag to his friend, "I need help with tying and zipping."

"I know." Rex smiled. "I'm happy to help you. Then *I* will need *your* help with buttons and buckles."

Rex zipped Drag into his snowsuit. He tied his boots and hat.

Then Drag tried to help Rex, but he was too bundled up. So Rex unzipped Drag's snowsuit and pulled off Drag's mittens.

"That's better," said Drag. "Now I can help you."

He buckled Rex's boots, buttoned him up, and put his own mittens back on. "Let's go!"

But now Drag was unzipped.

Rex tried to zip up Drag, but he was too bundled up. So Drag unbuttoned Rex and pulled off Rex's mittens.

"That's better," said Rex. Then he rezipped Drag. "Ready!"

But now Rex was unbuttoned.

So Rex unzipped Drag so he could help rebutton his coat.

Then Drag unbuttoned Rex so he could zip him up again.

Finally, Rex said, "Wait. I have an idea."

He kicked off his boots and stepped out of his snowsuit.

Drag took off his boots and stepped out of *his* snowsuit.

Then Rex zipped himself into *Drag's* snowsuit and tied on *Drag's* boots. Drag buttoned himself into *Rex's* snowsuit and buckled on *Rex's* boots.

Drag yawned. "Getting ready to play in the snow is a lot of work."

Rex yawned. "Yes, it is."

They plopped themselves down on the floor and closed their eyes.

No need for blankets. They were perfectly warm and snug.

Chapter 2

Almost a Snowbear

"I found a pair of eyes!" Rex said.

Drag gasped. "Gross!"

"Not *real* eyes, silly dragon!" Rex said, shaking his enormous head. He held up two flat stones.

"Oh. Phew!" said Drag.

"Where's the carrot for the nose?" Rex asked.

"I ate it."

"Drag! Our snowbear needs a nose!"

Drag dug under the snow. "Here's one!"

"We don't want rocks for the eyes *and* the nose, do we?" Rex asked.

Drag dug in the snow some more. "How about this?" he asked, holding out an acorn.

Before Rex could say, *That will work*, Drag tossed the acorn into the air and opened his mouth to catch it.

Rex tried to snatch it, but his little arms couldn't reach. The acorn landed between Drag's teeth and . . . *CRUNCH!*

"That's the second nose you've eaten today!" Rex said.

"I'm sorry. Playing in the snow makes me hungry."

"Everything makes you hungry," Rex pointed out.

Drag searched around giant trees and between snowbanks. "Here's something we can use!" He picked up a branch with pine needles on the end. Drag tickled Rex's cheek, before sticking the branch into the middle of the snowbear's face.

"That's a very nice nose," Rex said.

"Yes. It smells piney. And I don't want to eat it!" Drag leaned in and sniffed the branch-nose. "AAAAAAAHHHH, AAAAAHHHH, ACHOOOOOOOOOO!"

Drag blushed. "Oopsie."

Rex stomped his foot. It made a big splash. "Drag! You melted all of the snow with your sneeze!"

"But now we have a lake!" Drag said happily. "Let's go swimming!"

Chapter 3

Fun at Last

"A lake in the winter is not fun," said Rex. "It's much too cold to swim."

"It *is* very cold," said Drag.

"We need snow!" said Rex. "We can't build anything with water!"

"We need a snowstorm," said Drag.

Rex and Drag looked up at the sky through the tops of the trees. They watched and watched. And watched some more.

"I think I see a snowflake!" said Drag.

"I don't see a snowstorm anywhere up there," said Rex. "That means no snowbears. No snowdinos. No snowforts. No snowdragons. No fun."

The wind blew.

Drag shivered.

Rex shivered.

Drag chattered loudly.

Rex chattered louder, because he had more teeth.

"I'm frozen." Rex's tail quivered.

"I feel frozen, too." Drag's shoulders shook.

"It's so cold," Rex complained.

Drag frowned.

Rex frowned. And then Rex smiled.

"Why are you smiling?" Drag asked his friend. "It's too cold to be happy!"

Rex's smile grew even bigger. "I'm happy because we have a lake."

"But you said it's too cold to swim!" Drag blew gently on his mittens to try to warm his claws.

"Yes, but it *is* cold enough for something else," said Rex, his smile wider still. "I'll help you with the tying."

They may have been short on snow,
but there was no shortage of fun.

The Scary Story

Chapter 1

Shhhh! I'm Reading

"Hi, Drag," Rex said.

Drag sat by the window in the den. "Shhhh . . . please. I'm reading," he said.

But before Rex made it into the kitchen to heat up some tea, Drag jumped up from his chair. His wings flapped and he coughed out a ring of smoke.

"Be careful!" Rex wheezed. He turned his face away.

"I'm sorry, but I am scared. And when I'm scared, I get jumpy. And flappy."

"And smoky," Rex said. He waved his little hands to clear the air. "What's scaring you?"

"Something I'm reading is *very* scary."

"What are you reading?" Rex asked.

"A book," said Drag, rolling his eyes.

"Yes, I know that." Rex sighed. "I meant, what are you reading *about* that's scary?"

"Oh. There's a monster in this story." Drag held the book out so Rex could see.

"What kind of monster?" Rex asked as he took the book from Drag.

"This monster is *huge*!" Drag pulled himself up to his full height.

"And?"

"It has pointy teeth!" Drag opened his mouth and gasped.

"And?"

"Sharp claws!" Drag clasped his own claws together.

Rex flipped through the pages of the book. He studied the cover.

"That's not all!" Drag continued. "The monster blows smoke rings out of its nose!"

"No kidding!" said Rex.

"I kid you not!" Drag snorted. A smoke ring floated over Rex's head and landed on his shoulders like a necklace. "I don't like books about monsters."

"Well," said Rex, holding the book out to Drag and pointing to the picture on the cover. "Since you don't like monsters, it's a very good thing your book is about a dragon."

Chapter 2

A Monster-ish Dragon

"This book is about a dragon?" Drag asked. He held the cover close to his face.

"Drag. How can you, a dragon yourself, not know that this is a book about a dragon?"

"Because *this* dragon looks monster-ish."

Rex shrugged. "He looks dragon-ish to me."

"But he looks too *mean* to be a dragon," Drag said.

Rex smiled at his friend. "I don't know any mean dragons," he said.

Drag thought for a moment. "I don't know any, either."

"I would not like to meet a mean dragon," said Rex.

"I wouldn't, either," said Drag. "They scare people."

"Why do you think the dragon on the book looks scary?" Rex asked. "Is it because he is so huge?"

"No."

"His pointy teeth?"

Drag shook his head.

"His sharp claws? His fire-y breath?"

"No and no."

"Then what did the book dragon *do* that is so monster-ish?" Rex asked.

Drag stretched his wings up so high, they knocked against the ceiling. "I can't tell you," he whined.

"Why not?"

"Because I don't know what happens in the story! I'm only on page one."

Chapter 3

Maybe Scary, Maybe Not

"Drag, *you* are huge," said Rex.

Drag stood up straight and puffed out his chest. "Yes. I am."

"You have pointy teeth and sharp claws."

"I do. I like my claws." Drag fanned his claws out in front of him and grinned.

"*You* have a long tail and scaly wings."

"That is a fact!" Drag tossed his head proudly.

He flapped his wings. He swooshed his tail. The curtains in the room fluttered.

"And *you* breathe fire once in a while, which certainly comes in handy!"

"A dragon has to do what a dragon has to do."

"Drag," Rex said, "*you* are not scary."

"Of course I'm not!"

"So maybe the dragon in your book isn't scary, either."

"But he looks so scary," said Drag, sounding doubtful. "He isn't smiling."

"Nobody smiles all of the time. Maybe he's tired," Rex offered.

"Oh," said Drag.

"Or maybe he's sad about something."

"I didn't think of that," Drag said, flipping through the book's pages.

"He could be worried or even . . . scared," Rex continued. "Maybe you should keep reading the book and find out."

"Rex?"

"Yes, Drag?"

"Shhhhhh, please. I'm reading."

Susan Lubner is the author of the middle grade novels *Lizzy and the Good Luck Girl* and *The Upside of Ordinary*, as well as several picture books, including *Noises at Night*, co-authored with Beth Raisner Glass, which was featured on *TODAY* as a "Best Book for Young Children." She lives in Massachusetts. Visit her online at SusanLubner.com.

Blythe Russo is the author-illustrator of *Sloth Sleeps Over*, and has illustrated several other picture books. She lives just outside Cincinnati, Ohio, holds a master's in illustration from the Savannah College of Art and Design, and is an active member of SCBWI. Visit her online at BlytheRussoIllustration.com.